THE KNIGHT WHO
WAS AFRAID TO FIGHT

Barbara Shook Hazen · Pictures by Toni Goffe

Dial Books for Young Readers New York

Published by Dial Books for Young Readers
A Division of Penguin Books USA Inc.
375 Hudson Street
New York, New York 10014

Designed by Nancy R. Leo
Printed in Hong Kong
by South China Printing Company (1988) Limited
First Edition
1 3 5 7 9 10 8 6 4 2

Library of Congress Cataloging in Publication Data
Hazen, Barbara Shook. The knight who was afraid to fight
by Barbara Shook Hazen ; pictures by Toni Goffe.
p. cm.
Summary: Sir Fred, considered to be the bravest knight in the castle,
fears for his reputation when a jealous bully tries to expose
his secret fear of fighting.
ISBN 0-8037-1591-9 (trade).—ISBN 0-8037-1592-7 (library)
[1. Knights and knighthood—Fiction.   2. Fear—Fiction.]
I. Goffe, Toni, ill.   II. Title.
PZ7.H314975Kp 1994   [E]—dc20   93-4608   CIP   AC

The art for this book was prepared with ink and watercolors.
It was then color-separated and reproduced as red, yellow, blue, and black halftones.

*For Brackish days and knightly feasts
around the Randall Roundtable*

B.S.H.

*For wonderful days, knights, and castles
with Rob, Kim, and Mikeala*

T.G.

Long ago in the days of knights, Sir Fred was said to be the boldest of the bold and the bravest of the brave—especially by the fair Lady Wendylyn.

This enraged Melvin the Miffed, the mean-spirited castle bully who was jealous of the noble knight.

    After a long, self-imposed exile, he returned, doubly determined to get the dirt on Sir Fred and to ruin his reputation for good. Melvin the Miffed sneaked and peeked about endlessly, searching for a crack in Sir Fred's armor.

One day, with a happy "Aha!" he observed that Sir Fred's sword was only grass-stained, not bloodied when Sir Fred returned from doing one of his knightly good deeds.

Later Melvin the Miffed watched as Sir Fred paled, pushed back his plate, and politely excused himself from the round table when the other knights gathered to boast of their bloody battles.

Perhaps Sir Fred was not so bold and brave as everyone thought? And if the sight of blood so bothered him, perhaps he was even afraid to fight?

Melvin the Miffed went up to his chamber and searched his
memory bank for instances of Sir Fred's failure to fight. He
recalled that Sir Fred had driven the monsters out of the castle
moat by tickling their tails rather than by beheading them.

He recalled how Sir Fred had saved Lady Wendylyn from the hideous ten-headed dragon: He had *fooled* it out of its frightful feast rather than thrusting his sword down its ten terrible throats.

To test his theory Melvin the Miffed smeared Sir Fred's nightcap with ketchup, which sent the good knight screaming from his bedchamber.

Melvin the Miffed then poured red plant dye into the bathwater, which sent Sir Fred out into the night, crying, "It's a bloodbath!"

After that the rumors about Sir Fred's flaw flew. So did a banner demanding, "What good knight—whose name rhymes with *red*—doesn't like to fight?"

Lady Wendylyn saw the banner and winced. Quickly she dismissed the dark thought that crossed her mind. She turned her attention to a love letter from Sir Fred. Melvin the Miffed seized the opportunity to plant a wicked seed of doubt as he whispered, "Perhaps your not-so-bold-or-brave knight prefers the pen to the sword!"

The doubtful seed grew into a sapling as Lady Wendylyn recalled Sir Fred's refusal to swat a mosquito on her sleeve, and his pallor when he accidentally drew blood while trimming his pet falcon's toenails.

That evening Lady Wendylyn decided to test her True Love's bravery and boldness by demanding, "Fetch me the most perfect rose from the highest place."

"Gladly," Sir Fred said as he clambered up the royal trellis.

As he plucked, he pricked his finger. Still clutching the perfect rose, Sir Fred paled and fainted in his True Love's arms.

Lady Wendylyn fanned him furiously. Was what seemed a sign of lovesickness really a case of the cowardly queasies?

"What a sorry sight! Foolish Lady trying to revive Faint Heart!" snickered Melvin the Miffed, sneaking up on the couple.

"Did you hear what he said?" Lady Wendylyn's eyes flashed as she shook Sir Fred awake.

"I did," Sir Fred replied faintly.

"Well, what are you going to do about it?" Lady Wendylyn's temper rose.

"An insult is a fine excuse for a fight," Melvin the Miffed sneered. He licked his hairy lips and leered at Sir Fred.

Steadying himself, Sir Fred said, more calmly than he felt, "I have no intention of going to war over a silly insult. Sticks and stones may bruise my bones. Insults can't dent my armor."

"I don't give a fig about your armor. What about my honor? Aren't you going to defend it?" Lady Wendylyn demanded, tossing her curls and stamping her foot.

Sir Fred hestitated.

Melvin the Miffed didn't. He chortled with glee and flung his glove at Sir Fred's feet.

According to the Rules of Knighthood, a dropped glove is a challenge that must be met. Sir Fred was honor-bound to fight or lose his knighthood, his good reputation, and—far worse—his ladylove.

Sir Fred picked up the glove and sighed, "Tomorrow at sunrise."

"Yeah! Hooray!" whooped Melvin the Miffed.

"But I insist on blunted lances, so nobody will get hurt," Sir Fred
added in a trembling voice.

"Boo! Hiss!" Melvin the Miffed snorted.

"Wimp! Coward! Niddering Knight!" Lady Wendylyn said as
she flounced off in an angry snit.

That night Sir Fred did not have a good knight's sleep. He tossed and turned fitfully. His thoughts churned—about fleeing, about fighting, about being hurt. The worst, though, was being thought a coward by his True Love.

Lady Wendylyn was upset too. She shredded rose petals and bit her too-quick tongue. Then she sent Sir Fred a note of apology along with a good-luck token.

In the pre-dawn dark a forlorn Sir Fred polished his sword and slipped into his armor. Lady Wendylyn's gift arrived just as he was about to leave.

It was a golden mirror with a note that said, "Sorry about my snit."

Sir Fred sighed and put it over his heart.

Melvin the Miffed prepared himself for the duel too. He put a
poison tip on his lance and carried a pouch of killer bees. "Foul
play is more fun than fair," he told himself. "What weapons won't
do, stingers will."

Sir Fred and Melvin the Miffed met on the battlefield and prepared to draw straws. Whoever drew the short straw would have the sun in his eyes.

Melvin the Miffed drew it but Sir Fred gallantly insisted on trading, saying, "It is my knightly duty to be polite."

As the sun burst on the horizon, Melvin the Miffed and Sir Fred faced each other. To the sound of trumpets the herald shouted the battle cry, "Onward!"

Sir Fred and Melvin the Miffed each spurred his horse to a thunderous pace. The Rules of Duels were clear: The first one to unseat the other would be the winner. The winner could then punish or pardon the loser.

The bright sun blinded Sir Fred, who thrust his lance first. And missed.

Melvin the Miffed glowered, released the killer bees from their pouch, and aimed his poison-tipped lance straight at Sir Fred's heart.

As he did, the reflection of his own mean face in Lady Wendylyn's gift mirror blinded him and his horse too. It reared, unseating him, as his weapon fell into the cement-thick mud.

Melvin the Miffed landed on his own upended lance, hoist by the seat of his chain-mail underpants, with the killer bees in pursuit.

"Help!" Melvin the Miffed whimpered for mercy.

"Be off!" Sir Fred said as he held out his own blunt-tipped sword to a red-faced Melvin the Miffed. "For foul play you deserve to dangle, but not to die."

Then he turned to Lady Wendylyn and told her, "It is true. The sight of blood makes me sick. It is also true—I do not like to fight, most of all with you. If that makes me less than a good knight, then I have won the battle but lost your love."

"Never!" Lady Wendylyn replied, flinging herself into her True Love's arms. "I love you as you are, even if we don't always agree. Forgive me, I was foolish to pick a fight over a silly insult."

"You certainly were!" Sir Fred faced his True Love fearlessly. Then he kissed her and they cantered off together into the rosy morning.